TABLE OF CONTENTS

KIRSTEN

A nine-year-old who moves with her family to a new home on America's frontier in 1854.

PAPA, LARS, MAMA, AND PETER

The Larsons sometimes long for Sweden, but they never lose heart for the challenges of pioneer life.

THE BOOKS ABOUT KIRSTEN

♥

MEET KIRSTEN · An American Girl

Kirsten and her family make the difficult journey from Sweden to begin a new life on the Minnesota frontier.

♥

KIRSTEN LEARNS A LESSON · A School Story

Kirsten must learn English at school. She learns an important lesson from her secret Indian friend, too.

♥

KIRSTEN'S SURPRISE · A Christmas Story

Kirsten and Papa travel to town to get their trunk from Sweden. Their errand turns into a terrifying trip.

♥

HAPPY BIRTHDAY, KIRSTEN! · A Springtime Story

After taking care of Mama and the new baby, Kirsten gets a birthday surprise during the Larsons' barn raising.

♥

KIRSTEN SAVES THE DAY · A Summer Story

Kirsten and Peter find honey in the woods, but their discovery leads to a dangerous adventure.

♥

CHANGES FOR KIRSTEN · A Winter Story

A raccoon causes a disaster for the Larsons, but Kirsten and Lars find a treasure that means better times.

HAPPY
BIRTHDAY,
KIRSTEN!
A SPRINGTIME STORY

BY JANET SHAW

ILLUSTRATIONS RENÉE GRAEF

VIGNETTES KEITH SKEEN

PLEASANT COMPANY

Published by Pleasant Company Publications
© Copyright 1987 by Pleasant Company

First Edition.
Printed in the United States of America.
95 96 97 98 99 RND 31 30 29 28 27

PICTURE CREDITS
The following individuals and organizations have generously given
permission to reprint illustrations contained in "Looking Back":
pp. 54-55—International Museum of Photography at George Eastman
House; Matthew Isenburg; State Historical Society of Wisconsin;
pp. 56-57–Gernsheim Collection, Harry Ransom Humanities Research Center,
The University of Texas at Austin; Early Settler Life Series, Crabtree
Publishing Company, 350 Fifth Avenue, Suite 3308, New York, NY
10118; Early Settler Life Series, Crabtree Publishing Company, New York;
Early Settler Life Series, Crabtree Publishing Company, New York; Early
Settler Life Series, Crabtree Publishing Company, New York; Early Settler
Life Series, Crabtree Publishing Company, New York; pp. 58-59–Early
Settler Life Series, Crabtree Publishing Company, New York; Early Settler
Life Series, Crabtree Publishing Company, New York; Early Settler Life
Series, Crabtree Publishing Company, New York; Early Settler Life Series,
Crabtree Publishing Company, New York; Matthew Isenburg;
International Museum of Photography at George Eastman House.

Edited by Jeanne Thieme
Designed by Myland McRevey
Art Directed by Kathleen A. Brown

Library of Congress Cataloging-in-Publication Data

Shaw, Janet Beeler, 1937–
Happy birthday, Kirsten!: a springtime story

(The American girls collection)
Summary: On a Minnesota farm in the mid 1800's, the hard working
members of the Larson family find time to celebrate Kirsten's tenth birthday.
[1. Frontier and pioneer life–Fiction.   2. Swedish Americans–
Fiction.   3. Birthdays–Fiction]
I. Graef, Renee, ill.   II. Title.   III. Series.
PZ7.S53423Hap 1987   [Fic]   87-12208
ISBN 0-937295-88-4
ISBN 0-937295-33-7 (pbk.)

FOR MY MOTHER,
NADINA FOWLER

MISS WINSTON
*Kirsten's teacher,
who lives with
Uncle Olav's family.*

ANNA, AUNT INGER, LISBETH, AND UNCLE OLAV
*Kirsten's American relatives live on a new farm in Minnesota, where they
make the Larson family feel at home.*

TORNADO!

"Hit your rug harder!" Anna called to Kirsten. "Look, I can make more dust fly than you can!"

"It makes me sneeze," Kirsten said. But she liked smacking the rag carpets that Mama and Aunt Inger had draped over the line. She grinned as she slapped the dirt out with a small branch from the maple tree.

Anna held her branch with both hands. Because she was only eight, the youngest of the girls, she'd been given the smallest rug. The tip of her nose was as pink as a cherry blossom from the sun and the work.

After the long winter the clothes, bedding, and

rugs were full of dirt and soot, but Kirsten and Anna laughed and chattered as they beat the rugs. Lisbeth called "Hello!" as she brought bed linens from the big house to where Mama and Aunt Inger were doing the laundry. They were all so glad it was warm enough to be outside.

The Larsons' first winter in America had been bitterly cold, but at last the deep snows of Minnesota melted. Now May greened the farm Kirsten's family shared with Uncle Olav and Aunt Inger. Papa, Lars, and Uncle Olav were working the fields so they could plant wheat and corn. As soon as the seed was in the ground the men would raise a new barn. That would be wonderful, Kirsten thought—a big new barn and a barn-raising party. But first there was so much work to be done.

Kirsten sneezed again and stopped to wipe her nose on the corner of her apron. The strong wind off the prairie whipped her skirt around her legs and pulled Anna's braids straight back from her head. It fanned the flames under the steaming laundry kettle where Mama and Aunt Inger stirred the sheets.

As Peter brought the cows in to be milked, his

cap blew off his head and tumbled across the barn
lot. Mama scooped up the cap as it rolled to her
feet, then looked at the sky in alarm.

Kirsten looked, too. All day the sun had shone,
but now the sky was getting dark as though night
were coming early. Mama waved Kirsten to her
side. She put her wet, warm hand on Kirsten's
shoulder. "Those black clouds worry me," Mama
said.

Aunt Inger shaded her eyes to study the
horizon. "Another tornado might be coming,"
she said. "Last spring a tornado ripped up
the woodlot and almost took that old barn.
We should go into the root cellar to be safe."

Even as Aunt Inger spoke, the wind blew
several shingles off the roof of the little barn. "Get
your brother and your cousins, Kirsten," Mama
said. "Hurry!"

The wind shoved Kirsten as she ran to the barn
lot. "Come quickly!" she called to Lisbeth and Anna.
"That might be a tornado!" The pine trees thrashed,
the tall grass flattened, and the wind howled as
black clouds sped toward the farm. If a tornado
touched down here, it could destroy the house and

"Get your brother and your cousins, Kirsten," Mama said.
"Another tornado might be coming."

the cabin and the barn and everything in them. It could carry away the pieces of the new barn that hadn't even been put up yet. Kirsten grabbed Peter's hand. "A tornado! We have to get underground to be safe! Come to the root cellar!"

No one had to be told twice to hide from a tornado. Peter picked up the gray cat, Missy, and ran after Kirsten. Mama was already at the back of the big house, opening the door to the root cellar. Anna and Lisbeth scrambled in like prairie dogs into a burrow. Aunt Inger came with a lantern and the family Bible in her arms. Right behind her ran Miss Winston, the schoolteacher who was staying with the Larsons. She held a quilt over her head and shoulders like a cloak.

Peter skidded into the root cellar with Kirsten right behind him. Then Mama and Miss Winston crowded in, and Aunt Inger dragged the door shut behind her and bolted it tightly.

"Where are Lars and Papa and Uncle Olav?" Kirsten asked.

"They're helping at the Peterson farm today, but don't worry. The men will lie down in a ditch if they see a funnel cloud coming," Aunt Inger said.

"Here, turn over a bucket and sit down." She lit the lantern and set it by her feet.

Everyone huddled together shoulder to shoulder in the little room dug out of the earth under the house. Last fall the root cellar had been packed full of potatoes, turnips, carrots, beets, and apples. During the winter the families had eaten almost all the vegetables. Now there were only a few wrinkled apples left. Aunt Inger picked them up and handed them around. "These will have to be our lunch," she said. "We can't go out until the danger is past."

Aunt Inger held the family Bible in her lap—it was the most important thing the Larsons owned. Every night Uncle Olav or Papa read from it. In the front of the Bible the names and important dates for everyone in the whole family were written. Kirsten liked to read her own birthday there:

Kirsten Larson, born June 8, 1845, Ryd, Sweden

In a month she would be ten years old.

Kirsten was too nervous to eat the apple Aunt Inger had given her. Outside, the wind roared and howled like the train that had brought her family across the country to their new home. What would they do if the tornado blew their cabin away? And Mama was going to have a baby soon—where would the baby be born if they didn't have a home? Kirsten pressed against Mama's side.

Miss Winston pulled her quilt from her head and smoothed her hair. "In Maine we never ever had a tornado. No one will believe me when I write home about these dangers!" But she smiled to show them that a ship captain's daughter knew how to be brave.

Anna touched the corner of Miss Winston's quilt. "Couldn't you find your cloak?" she asked. Anna was never too scared to be curious.

"I never thought about my cloak! I just knew I had to save my quilt, so I took it and ran." Miss Winston sat up straight like a lady and smoothed the quilt in her lap. "Every time I look at my quilt, it's like getting a letter from home."

"You were right to save it," Aunt Inger said. "It's beautiful!"

Kirsten had often seen the brightly colored quilt on Miss Winston's bed, but she'd never looked at it closely. Now she leaned forward to study it. It was white, and covered with designs that looked like wreaths of flowers. Each design was made from small pieces of fabric. The whole quilt was sewn with tiny, perfect stitches, the kind of stitches Mama was teaching Kirsten to make.

"It must have taken a long time to sew," Lisbeth said. She was twelve, and her sewing was already like a grown woman's.

Anna shuddered when the wind huffed at the door. "Did you make your quilt, Miss Winston?" she asked in a small voice.

"Oh, no! Shall I tell you how this quilt was made?" Miss Winston said.

Anna nudged Kirsten's foot with hers, because Miss Winston never missed a chance to teach a lesson. "Yes, please," Anna said.

"It did take a long time to sew," Miss Winston said proudly. "My mother and my aunts and cousins and my sister made this quilt for me. They gave it to me to remember them by when I left

home." She pointed to the flower designs in the quilt. "The pink cloth in the center of this flower is from my sister's old apron. The cloth in this green leaf is from a dress of my mother's. The yellow cloth for the flower petals came from a dress I wore as a baby."

It was hard for Kirsten to imagine Miss Winston as a baby, but she liked the quilt's lively colors. They made her think of the wildflowers in the meadow.

"Everyone who helped make this quilt signed her name to it," Miss Winston said. "It's a friendship quilt." Her eyes had a faraway look, as though she were gazing at her friends and family back in Maine instead of the dirt walls of the damp root cellar.

"Do you think you could teach us to sew a quilt?" Kirsten asked. Whenever she admired something she wanted to do it herself.

"Yes, could you?" Lisbeth echoed.

Miss Winston raised her eyebrows. "Haven't I taught you sums and reading and recitation and penmanship? Of course I can teach you to make a quilt! A big one like mine would be difficult, but you could each make a small square. I have some white muslin in my trunk. I'll cut three pieces for the background."

Anna nudged Kirsten's foot again as the girls

looked at each other excitedly. "But what can we use for making the designs?" Kirsten asked.

"You'll need only small bits of cloth for that," Miss Winston said. "Just scraps will do."

"We can use my worn-out kerchief," Anna said.

"And scraps from the ragbag," Lisbeth added.

"My apron can't be patched anymore. We could cut it up for scraps," Kirsten said.

Mama put her hand on Kirsten's knee. "You don't have time for fancy sewing," she said. "Remember, I need all your help to make clothes for the baby." She patted her big belly to remind Kirsten that it wouldn't be long now until they'd need the baby things.

Kirsten sighed. It was tiresome to hem shirts and diapers for the baby Mama was expecting. Why did a baby need so many diapers? Surely three or four would be enough.

"But quilting trains the hand and eye," Miss Winston said sternly, as though Mama were one of her pupils, too. "And a quilt is so practical. Mine is wonderfully warm."

Mama looked doubtful. Quilting was something

new to her. The Swedish women wove their
blankets and bedcoverings on looms.

"Maybe Lisbeth and I could learn and teach
you when you have time, Kirsten," Anna said.

"I bet you'll still be able to sew just before
bedtime," Lisbeth said. "And at school we can sew
during recess. I know the other girls would like to
do it, too."

"Sewing at recess, what a good idea!" Miss
Winston said. "After you walk about and take deep
breaths, I'm sure there will be a little time left for
sewing. Where there's a will there's always a way."

11

She wrapped her quilt around her shoulders again.

The gray cat jumped from Peter's lap and curled around Kirsten's ankles. Missy was going to have kittens soon and didn't like to be fussed over now. But Kirsten felt comforted when she petted the cat, so she stroked Missy's soft head. "I'll sew the baby things so fast that I know I'll have some time," she told Lisbeth and Anna.

"It's decided, then!" Lisbeth said. "We'll learn to make a quilt."

"Who knows what these girls will learn next!" Aunt Inger said to Mama. Then she cocked her head. While they'd been talking, the wind had died down. "I think it might be safe to go out now," she said. "Let's look."

She lifted the heavy bolt. The small door swung open onto a patch of sky as blue as one of the pieces in Miss Winston's quilt. All the rugs and covers had blown off the lines, and a few shingles had blown off the rooftops. Broken branches littered the barn lot. But both houses and the old barn stood safe in the clearing among the pines.

Mama let out a long sigh, as though she'd been holding her breath. "Thank God that this danger has passed us by," she said. They crept out of the root cellar like bears out of a cave, into the fresh air.

CHAPTER
TWO
―

NEW BABIES

School started again for the summer, and all the girls gathered at recess every day to sew. Kirsten liked to lean against the sun-warmed logs of the schoolhouse and chatter with her friends. They had traded scraps of cloth so that everyone could make a colorful design on a square of white muslin. The designs they made from the bits of cloth slowly grew in their hands the way wild violets bloomed on the prairie.

Mary Stewart, whose family had come to Minnesota from Boston, was making the fanciest design. Mary had worked on a quilt before, so when Miss Winston wasn't there to give directions

14

she helped the others sew difficult corners and curves. She had beautiful curly brown hair and a squinched-up face like a sleepy puppy's.

Today Mary was showing Kirsten how to make a sharp corner. Her curls brushed Kirsten's braids as they bent over a small piece of blue cloth. "This is a piece of linen my mother wove," Kirsten said. "There was just a tiny bit left after she made a shirt for Papa. Now all she makes are baby clothes. She's making little caps from an old pillowcase."

Mary wet her finger and knotted a piece of thread. "Last year my Aunt Sadie had twins. Only one of the babies lived, and Aunt Sadie died after they were born."

Kirsten made herself concentrate on Mary's quick fingers and the flashing needle. She didn't want to think that Mama was in danger.

"My mother took Aunt Sadie's baby to raise. We call her my little sister, but she's really my cousin. She never knew her real mother, of course," Mary went on, her lips pursed over her sewing.

Kirsten pricked her finger on her needle and sucked hard at the hurt place. Everyone seemed to know stories of mothers or babies who had died

"Last year my Aunt Sadie had twins," said Mary.
"Only one of the babies lived."

here on the frontier. To think of something happening to Mama made Kirsten want to cry. It was better not to think of that. It was much better to think about the pretty designs they were making.

Anna had left the sewing circle to ask Miss Winston to untangle her thread. Now she came running back. Gladly, Kirsten made a place for Anna to sit between her and Mary. Anna pulled her quilt square from her apron pocket. "Honestly, isn't Miss Winston the nicest teacher ever? I'll be sorry when she has to leave Powderkeg School."

Kirsten was startled. She thought Miss Winston would be with them always, like family. "Why would she want to leave?" Kirsten asked.

"Teachers always move on," Mary said. "I've been at this school for four years and we've had four different teachers. Miss Winston is the only nice one."

Anna picked a little white flower that bloomed in the shelter of the log school and held it to her nose. "Miss Winston likes it here. She often says so."

"I hope she stays!" Kirsten said. She wished that everything would stay just like it was now. The morning light was sweet and clear, the woods were green again, and they were all happy to have Miss Winston with them. If only Mama felt better—that was the one thing Kirsten would change. These days Mama was as nervous and irritable as Missy, the gray cat.

"If Miss Winston does leave, maybe we could add our squares to her quilt. Then she'd remember us, too," Anna said. "I can imagine her saying, 'This piece of brown calico is Anna's. This blue linen is Kirsten's.'"

"And, 'This red cotton is Mary's,'" Mary added quickly. "But Miss Winston's quilt is finished. When she showed it to us, I saw the fancy border."

Kirsten had an idea. "We could make another quilt for Miss Winston. And we could all sign our names to it, just the way her family did. Then when she looks at it, she'll think of all of us."

Anna smiled right away. She jumped to her feet and pranced around the circle, lifting her knees like a little pony. "That's a grand idea!" she said.

But Mary frowned. "It takes a long time to make a quilt. We can't make one in a rush."

Kirsten pressed her lips together tightly. Oh,

she knew Mary was right. It had taken several days just to cut out a design. Sewing it to the background was taking even longer. And making all the tiny quilting stitches would surely take weeks. Now that there was so much work to do at home, Kirsten had no time to work on her design before bed. Some days Mama's back ached so badly that Kirsten had to stay home from school to help her bake and cook. On those days, Kirsten didn't even get to sew at recess.

Still, Kirsten wouldn't give up her plan to make a quilt. "We could sew all of our squares together and make a small one," she said. "If we worked fast, we could finish it before the summer term is over."

"I think we should try," Lisbeth agreed in her slow voice that meant she was serious. She liked to think things through, so when she said they'd try, Kirsten thought the quilt was as good as finished.

But Mary sat back on her heels. She shook her brown curls like a wet dog shaking off water. "No, no, no!"

Kirsten was surprised. "Why not at least try?" she asked.

Mary folded her arms and shook her head again. "You don't understand. Being finished with the quilt isn't the best part," she said firmly. "*Making* the quilt is the best part. Anyway, that's what I like best—sewing it, all of us together."

Kirsten looked at Mary with new respect. Of course Mary was right. When the quilt was finished, the fun of working together would be over. And to be working and talking with her friends made Kirsten happy. "Yes," she said. "You're right, Mary."

Anna stood behind Kirsten. "I love your design!" she said. "It looks just like a heart."

"It's really a flower," Kirsten said. "I want it to look like the flowers Mama gave me to wear in my hair when I turned eight. We didn't celebrate my birthday when I turned nine. We were on our way from Sweden then."

"Then I'm sure you'll have a big celebration this year," Mary said. "Ten is a much more important birthday than nine, anyway."

Kirsten licked her thread and threaded her needle. Maybe she wouldn't celebrate her birthday this year, either. Maybe Mama had forgotten about her birthday. Mama had so much work to do for the new baby, and so much on her mind these days. Kirsten wanted to remind Mama, but she thought it was better not to bother her until after the baby was born. It was better just to help out all she could and pray that Mama would be well.

❤

Helping out meant more and more work for Kirsten. The cows gave more milk in the spring, so there was cheese to make and butter to churn. The chickens were laying again, and Kirsten had to feed them and gather eggs. She picked berries and greens to eat, too, and cooked breakfast and dinner when Mama wasn't able to be on her feet. Every night when her chores were done, Kirsten went straight to bed and fell asleep. And as soon as she woke in the morning, she started on that day's tasks. There was no time for sewing now.

One morning, as Kirsten was milking the cows with Aunt Inger, Lisbeth burst into the barn. "Come see Missy's new kittens!" she cried.

"What are you doing here, Lisbeth? You're supposed to be cooking breakfast," Aunt Inger said sternly. "The men will be in from the fields soon. They'll be hungry."

"I *was* cooking. Then Anna brought the eggs in, and she said that Missy was having her kittens. So I came out to see them. They're so small they look like mice." Lisbeth wiped her hand on her apron and made herself talk more slowly. "Kirsten, maybe you could come take a quick peek. The kittens have made a home in a pile of straw."

Kirsten looked at Aunt Inger, who nodded but didn't smile. Milk hissed into her bucket in two white streams. "Go on then, but be fast about it," Aunt Inger said. "We've still got two cows waiting."

Kirsten jumped up and followed Lisbeth. The sun was just rising, as pink as a primrose. The scent of lilacs and freshly turned earth was in the air. In the barn lot, Anna and Peter crouched beside a pile of straw near a huge wooden beam for the new barn. There was Missy, curled around her five baby kittens.

Missy licked and licked the kittens, which crawled blindly against her belly to look for milk. Two of the kittens were black and white, two were gray and white, and the smallest one was gray, just

like Missy. The gray kitten was so small it couldn't squeeze in to find a place to nurse. Instead, it bumped up against the beam, then against Missy's hind leg.

"That one's so little it will never live," Peter said. He'd heard Uncle Olav say that about one of the piglets.

"Be quiet, Peter," Kirsten said. "You don't know everything." She tried to guide the tiny gray kitten to its mother. But the kitten couldn't find its way.

"I think it has a chance," Lisbeth said. "Though

sometimes those very little ones aren't strong enough to make it."

Kirsten touched the gray kitten's stomach with the tip of her finger. The kitten's heart beat like the flutter of a butterfly wing. Its tiny mouth closed around her fingertip. Kirsten moved the kitten closer to Missy. "Oh, yes, that kitten will make it," Kirsten whispered. "You'll see."

"You like that one best, don't you?" Peter said. Kirsten nodded.

"Well, I like that black and white one," Peter said. He liked the puppies that were the toughest and the calves that were the biggest, too.

"I've got to finish milking with Aunt Inger," Kirsten said. "Peter, you make sure the gray kitten doesn't get lost in the grass, will you?"

Peter stood up and shoved his hands into his pockets the way their big brother Lars did. "Missy will take care of her kittens. She doesn't need help."

But Kirsten wasn't sure. That gray kitten was so very, very small. She leaned down to pet it one more time and whispered, "Be careful. Don't wander away or a hawk might get you. Drink lots

of milk. I'll come back to see you later." She
wanted to stay to guard it, but instead she ran back
to the barn to help Aunt Inger.

CHAPTER
THREE

—

BIG ENOUGH

"Kirsten! Kirsten!" Mama was calling from their cabin. It was late morning, and Kirsten and Lisbeth were straining cheese curds in the shed next to the big house. Kirsten put down the strainer and went to see what Mama wanted.

In the dim cabin, Mama sat on the edge of the bed. Her hands were pressed against her big belly. There was sweat on her forehead, and she looked worried. "Where's your Aunt Inger?" she asked.

"She took a pot of soup to the Petersons because they've been so sick. She'll be back by noontime," Kirsten said.

"And where's Papa?"

26

"He and Uncle Olav are helping Mr. Peterson finish his planting." Kirsten looked at her mother curiously. Why was Mama asking all these questions? She knew as well as Kirsten what work had to be done today. She was the one who had told Kirsten and Lisbeth to strain cheese curds.

"They'll be back soon, won't they?" Mama asked.

"Yes, Mama. They'll be back in time for lunch. Is something wrong?"

Mama patted the bed beside her. "Sit with me for a little while and keep me company. I think the baby is going to be born sooner than I expected. Maybe even today."

Kirsten's heart sped up and her mouth went dry. "Shouldn't I go fetch Aunt Inger to help you?"

"She'll be back soon. Just let me lie down and rest," Mama said.

Kirsten got the extra blanket and put it over Mama. Then she sat down beside her on the bed. Mama laced her fingers through Kirsten's. "Do you know what I thought about when I woke this morning?" Mama asked. Her eyes were a soft blue like the morning sky.

"What did you think about, Mama?"

Mama squeezed Kirsten's hand. "I remembered the day you were born, Kirsten. I remembered how my mother came to help me. Mrs. Hanson came, too. She helped all of us when we had babies. It was this time of year, late spring. New leaves were on the big maple tree outside the door. Then you were born, and Mrs. Hanson cleaned you and wrapped you in a blanket and put you in my arms. You were a red-faced little thing with white fuzz for hair. But I thought you were beautiful. I was so very, very happy because I wanted a daughter so much."

Kirsten put her head on her mother's shoulder. "Well, here I am," she said.

"Yes, here you are!" Mama smoothed the hair back from Kirsten's forehead. "And I was also thinking," Mama went on, stroking Kirsten's head, "that your birthday will be two weeks from this very day. June eighth. I'll never forget the day you were born."

So Mama did remember her birthday. How foolish Kirsten had been to think she would forget.

Suddenly, Mama squeezed Kirsten's hand extra

hard. Kirsten sat up straight. "Are you all right, Mama?"

"This baby wants to be born whether we're ready or not. We'd better not wait for Inger to come home. You'd better go fetch her, and Papa, too."

"Can't I help you here?" Kirsten asked. Her heart was racing.

"Get Lisbeth to stay with me," Mama said. "You go for Aunt Inger and Papa. Will you do that for me?" Mama wiped the sweat from her face with a corner of the blanket.

"I'll take Blackie. I'll ride as fast as an Indian, Mama! I'll be right back with Aunt Inger and Papa! I promise!"

As Kirsten ran across the yard she called, "Lisbeth, Mama's baby is coming and she needs you! Go quickly!" Then Kirsten dashed to the barn, grabbed Blackie's bridle, and chased him in from the pasture. "We have to hurry, Blackie!" she said as she pressed the bit between the horse's teeth. She climbed up the fence and onto his back.

Blackie liked to run. When Kirsten turned him into the lane and kicked him, he took off like a prairie fire. Kirsten leaned forward, and Blackie's

mane whipped her face. She held on to his mane
and the reins, and guided him with her knees. It
wasn't far to the Petersons' cabin, maybe only two
or three miles.

"Come on!" Kirsten urged the horse. Blackbirds
swooped up from the fields as they passed.
Blackie's hooves on the dirt lane pounded like a
second heartbeat. "Let Mama be all right!" Kirsten
prayed. "Please, let her be all right!"

Kirsten began calling, "Aunt Inger! Aunt Inger!"
as she rode up to the Petersons' cabin. Aunt Inger
was at the doorway in a moment.

"Is it your mama's time?" she asked.

"She says to come quickly. Oh, Aunt Inger,
please go as fast as you can!"

But Aunt Inger was already on her way,
running more than walking, taking the short cut
across the fields. "Your father and the others are
near the creek," she called over her shoulder. "And
don't worry. Your mama is strong and healthy."

Kirsten couldn't help but worry. She turned
Blackie to guide him down to the creek. Blackie
couldn't gallop on this rocky path, but he trotted as
if he knew they were on an important errand. Pine

"Oh, Aunt Inger," Kirsten said,
"please go as fast as you can!"

31

branches switched Kirsten's arms and shoulders.
She ducked low along Blackie's warm back, riding
the way the Indians rode their ponies.

Then they were in the plowed field and Kirsten
saw Papa. "Papa! Mama wants you!" she yelled as
she galloped across the field. "The baby's coming!"

"Is it that much of a hurry?" he said.

"Yes! You take the horse, Papa."

Papa gave Kirsten's shoulder a squeeze. He
said, "You're a good helper, Kirsten," as he hoisted
himself up on the horse's back.

Uncle Olav called, "Good luck!" as Papa took
off for the cabin. Kirsten and Uncle Olav followed
on foot.

"Let's run!" Kirsten said. "I want to help
Mama, too!"

"Walking will get us there fast enough,
Kirsten," Uncle Olav said kindly. "You're too young
to be in the cabin anyway. Inger and your father
will do what's needed for your mama. You wait
with Lisbeth and Anna at our house. There's plenty
for you to do there."

So Kirsten went back to the big house, where
Lisbeth heated soup and sliced bread and cheese for

the noon meal. But how could Kirsten eat when Mama was having the baby? She picked at her food. Waiting was so hard.

"We'd all better get on with what we have to do," Uncle Olav said after he finished his soup. "Babies come when they're ready. We can't hurry this one by worrying."

The afternoon crept along. Kirsten washed up the bowls and then fed the pigs and chickens. She was picking feathers from a wild turkey Lars had shot when she saw Aunt Inger in the doorway of the cabin. Aunt Inger waved her apron like a flag. And she was smiling!

Kirsten and Peter leaped like jack rabbits across the pasture. As they came to the door of the cabin, Kirsten took Peter's hand. He was trembling like a newborn calf. "Is Mama all right?" he blurted before Aunt Inger had a chance to say a word.

But Kirsten knew from Aunt Inger's smile that the news was good. "Come see for yourselves," Aunt Inger said and stood aside.

Kirsten and Peter tiptoed into the cabin. The sunlight made a path across the floor to the big bed where Mama lay.

She held out her hand to them. "Come see your little sister," she said.

There in the wooden cradle lay a little bundle in a blanket. Kirsten bent down. She saw a tiny pink face under a wisp of hair like yellow duck down.

"I thought a baby would be bigger," Peter said softly.

"Babies start out very small," Mama said. "But she's big enough." She reached up and ruffled his fair hair.

Peter grinned. "She's big enough," he repeated.

"Oh, Mama!" Kirsten breathed. Suddenly all of the extra energy went out of her. She wished she could just curl up on the bed beside Mama and rest, too.

"Now there are six of us," Mama said.

"Another mouth to feed," Papa said. He was smiling his biggest smile. "But all six of us are safe and well, thank the Lord."

PARTY PLANS

"How soon are we going to raise the
barn?" Peter asked. These days he
always said "we" when he talked
about the men's work. Papa was even teaching him
to split wood with the small axe.

Papa, Peter, and Lars sat at the table eating the
rabbit stew Kirsten had made for their supper. "We
plan to raise it a week from next Thursday, if the
weather is good," Papa said. "The other farmers
will come as soon as they've done their morning
chores. They'll bring their families with them, of
course. There will be nine men, plus Olav and Lars.
That should be enough." Papa had explained
several times how the men would pull up the big

beams and posts to make the barn. The beams were
so long and heavy that Kirsten couldn't imagine
how they would be raised. But it seemed that Papa
and Uncle Olav could do anything.

Kirsten dished up a serving of stew for Mama,
who rested in the bed with the baby. Mama wasn't
strong enough to work for very long yet, so Kirsten
did most of Mama's kitchen and farm chores. And
there were new chores, too. Several times each day,
Kirsten washed out the baby's diapers and hung
them to dry on the line outside.
With all her work, Kirsten had no
time to go to school. How lonely it
was on the farm when Anna and
Lisbeth were away all day. It seemed like years
since Kirsten had sat in that sunny spot behind the
schoolhouse, sewing with her friends. Every day
she was home, she imagined them working on their
squares without her. How she missed them and the
fun of making the quilt.

"Your friends from school will be here for the
barn raising," Mama said when she took her bowl
of stew from Kirsten. "They'll be coming with their
parents. Each family will bring food, and Inger is

going to make a huge kettle of venison stew for
everyone."

That pleased Kirsten, though she didn't see
how she'd have time to play with the other girls.
She'd probably have to help Mama with the extra
work.

"The families will be here all day, and after
supper we'll have music and dancing," Mama went
on. "I can't dance yet, but you and the others can."
Mama didn't seem to mind about the dancing. She
was smiling down at the baby who slept beside her.

Mama tugged Kirsten's braid. "I have something to ask you, dear."

Kirsten sighed. More work to do, she was sure.
"Yes, Mama," she said obediently.

"Our barn raising will be on the day before
your birthday. I thought you might like to do
something special when your friends are here,"
Mama said. "You've done the work of two women
lately, and you deserve a day to play."

Kirsten took Mama's hand. "A whole day with
my friends?"

Mama smiled. "Your tenth birthday should be a
day of your own. A day to celebrate and have fun."

Kirsten thought about picking wildflowers and playing games. And maybe there would be a cake to share. A barn raising and a birthday celebration, too! "May I run tell Lisbeth and Anna about it?" she asked Mama.

Papa started to say something about washing up, but Mama said, "Dishes can wait."

"I'll be right back," Kirsten said and scooted out the door.

As Kirsten ran to the other house, a wood thrush called and another answered from the pines. A thrush's song had never seemed such a happy melody as it did this evening. Kirsten tapped on the door, and Anna and Lisbeth came outside with her.

"They're coming! And it will be my birthday and a party!" Kirsten cried.

Lisbeth wiped her hands on her apron and said, "Slow down. Start over. Who's coming?"

Kirsten caught her breath. "On the day the men raise the barn, all our friends from school will be here. Mama says I can celebrate my birthday that day!"

"That's grand!" Anna said. She jumped up and down, her braids bouncing.

Lisbeth grabbed Kirsten's hand and swung it. "A party! Oh, that's wonderful news!"

"Mama says we'll be together all day and evening," Kirsten said. "We could work on our quilt for Miss Winston, too!"

Anna said, "But it's not for Miss—"

"Hush, Anna!" Lisbeth said. "It would be a perfect chance to work on the quilt, and you know it."

Anna blushed. "That's what I meant," she said.

"I'm way behind the rest of you with my sewing," Kirsten said. "It doesn't seem like I'm doing my part. But maybe I can catch up by then."

Anna put her arm around Kirsten's waist and looked up with a smile. "Oh, everyone knows you can't work on the quilt because you have to help your mama. It doesn't matter, truly it doesn't."

"It matters to me!" Kirsten said. "I miss the fun of doing it. And I miss being with all of you, too!" she blurted.

"On the day of your party, we'll sew as much as you want to," Lisbeth said.

Anna let go of Kirsten and hugged herself instead. "Oh, I can't wait for the surprise!"

"She means she can't wait for your party," Lisbeth said.

"I just wish I were going to be ten like you are, Kirsten!" Anna added.

FRIENDS COME
AROUND

"Pick as many daisies as you can!"
Anna told everyone. "We're going to
make daisy chains." All eight girls
fanned out across the meadow. It was the day of
the barn raising and they were picking wildflowers.

The day was clear and sunny, and Kirsten's
spirits swooped and soared like the bluebirds. She
stopped to look across the meadow to where the
men were working on the barn. Just after sunrise
they'd begun to haul the big beams up with strong
ropes, and by late morning there was the outline of
a barn where there had been only open sky. The
prairie didn't seem so wide with the new barn
there. Kirsten hoped Missy had kept her kittens out

of the way of the workers. Later, she'd look for the kittens. Now she buried her nose in the sweet-smelling bouquet she held.

When the girls had picked all the flowers they could carry, they took them back to Aunt Inger's house and decorated the big room with daisy chains. Then they sat outside under the dappled shade of the maple tree to sew. Kirsten had not finished the design on her square, but the other girls had finished theirs. When they laid them together on the grass, the squares made a lively pattern of blues, reds, greens, browns, and white. Mary arranged them. "We'll use a running stitch to join the squares. This part will go quickly," she said.

Kirsten hoped it wouldn't go too quickly. She knelt with her friends in a circle, chattering away as they joined their squares to make the top of a small quilt.

After the noon meal, the girls took up their sewing again. By the middle of the afternoon, they finished stitching the top of their quilt to a plain backing.

"This quilt isn't as large or heavy as the one

Kirsten knelt with her friends in a circle,
chattering away as they joined their squares.

Miss Winston has," Kirsten said.

"It's a summer coverlet," Mary explained. "No one had an extra blanket to sew between the layers."

"I'm sure Miss Winston will like it though," Kirsten added.

Anna giggled and hid her smile behind her hand.

"Anyway, *I* think it's lovely!" Kirsten went on. Now that she was with her friends again, she felt more strongly how much she'd missed them.

Mary was folding up the quilt when Aunt Inger called from the doorway, "Aren't you girls ready for some sweets?"

Everyone shouted "Yes!" at the same time and ran into the house. "Let me get Mama," Kirsten said. But Mama was already coming from the kitchen, carrying a heart-shaped cake. Kirsten caught her breath with pleasure.

Miss Winston clapped her hands and pretended to be stern. "Everyone must sit in a circle," she said.

"Happy birthday, Kirsten!" Lisbeth said. She placed a wreath of flowers on Kirsten's head. The

blossoms tickled Kirsten's ears through her
long hair. "Thank you, Lisbeth," she said.

"You look beautiful," Anna sighed.

"Now the cake!" Mama called.

When everyone was munching,
Aunt Inger said, "I have something
for your birthday, Kirsten."

She gave Kirsten a small package.
"New hair ribbons! Pink is my favorite
color. Thank you, Aunt Inger!"

Now Mama stepped forward. "And I made you
something pretty, for dress up." She handed Kirsten
a white apron with fancy trim around the edges.

"Oh, Mama, it's lovely!" Kirsten said. "But
when did you have time to make this?"

Miss Winston leaned close and whispered,
"Where there's a will there's always a way."

"I could wear this tonight at the barn-raising
dance, couldn't I?"

"You may wear it and the hair ribbons," Mama
smiled.

As Aunt Inger spooned strawberries into bowls
and covered them with fresh cream, Mary stood up,
brushed crumbs off her skirt, and straightened her

shoulders importantly. "Now *we* have something to give to Kirsten." She crossed the room, picked up the little quilt they had just finished sewing, and proudly handed it to Kirsten.

"Happy birthday, Kirsten. From all of us," she said.

Kirsten blinked. "Oh, thank you! But why are you giving this to me? It was for Miss Winston," she added in a whisper.

"I told the girls that one quilt is enough for anyone," Miss Winston said with a smile.

"And we're giving this one to you because you missed out on the fun of making it," Lisbeth explained. "We want you to know we didn't forget you, even when you weren't with us."

Anna took a corner of the quilt and spread it on the table. "See these plain squares? We put the plain ones in so we could write our names on them. Then it will be a friendship quilt, just like Miss Winston's."

Miss Winston took a quill pen and an inkpot from her school bag. "You must use your best handwriting," she directed the girls. "I don't want to see a single ink spot or smudge on this quilt."

Kirsten stroked the edge of her quilt as each girl took a turn signing her name on one of the plain squares. When all of the squares had been signed, Miss Winston wrote on the border of the quilt with her most beautiful writing:

For Kirsten Larson on her tenth birthday

It was late afternoon when the women began preparing supper. The men had finished raising the roof beams for the new barn, and now they used the extra boards to make wide tables. The girls set out pitchers of water and beer, and the women opened their baskets and laid out cheeses, breads, jam, butter, hams, roasted chickens, and cakes. The big pot of venison stew gave off a spicy scent. Everyone sat down to enjoy the feast, chatting and calling to one another as the sun began to set. Kirsten was almost too happy to be hungry. There would never be another day like this one, she was sure.

As the sky darkened, lanterns were hung on

the crossbeams of the barn. Some of the men took out fiddles, and the barn-raising dance began. Under the lanterns, the grownups danced to the tunes. Yankee tunes, German tunes, and Swedish tunes followed each other like the swirling dancers. The children made circle dances of their own around the edges. The full moon shone down through the open rafters like the biggest lantern of all.

Kirsten was skipping with Anna when she felt Papa's hand on her shoulder. "Come on, ten-year-old," Papa said in his deep voice. "This is your birthday dance with me."

The fiddlers were playing a spinning waltz. Papa clasped Kirsten firmly around her waist, she hung on to his shoulders, and they joined the grownups in the center of the new barn. Kirsten smelled Papa's good, clean sweat and the smell of new wood. Sometimes her feet left the floor when Papa swung her around, and the faces of the other dancers spun by like a moving daisy chain, but Papa guided her and kept her steady.

When the waltz was over, Kirsten was so excited she felt dizzy. Or maybe she'd just whirled

"Come on, ten-year-old," Papa said.
"This is your birthday dance with me."

around too many times. She left Papa and the crowd and went to rest on the back of one of the wagons. As she sat quietly in the moonlight, she saw Missy moving her kittens into the new barn. One by one, Missy lifted the kittens between the posts and into a dark corner. Kirsten counted four kittens. Where was the fifth one? Where was the little gray kitten?

Kirsten jumped up and went to look for it in the pile of straw where she'd seen them all before.

 She got down on her hands and knees and searched. Then she heard a tiny mew. There was the gray kitten! But Missy didn't seem to be coming back. Maybe she had given up on this kitten.

Kirsten took the kitten into her hand. She cupped it against her cheek and then snuggled it into the deep pocket of her new apron. She could feed it cow's milk, and it would grow strong. She would care for it, and it would live.

As Kirsten walked back to the new barn, the crowd began coming out. The men hitched their horses to the wagons. The women gathered up their baskets and sleepy children. Again and again, Papa and Uncle Olav thanked their neighbors. The women and girls hugged, then waved. "Good-bye! Good-bye! Good night!" echoed across the dark fields as the wagons pulled away.

Kirsten headed up to their cabin. When she opened the door, there was Mama, rocking the new baby in her cradle.

"Aren't you weary, Kirsten?" Mama asked. "Peter tried to stay awake, but you can see he fell asleep in his clothes."

Kirsten pulled her little stool next to Mama's chair. She liked the steady creak, creak the rocking cradle made. She took the kitten out of her pocket and showed it to Mama. "Missy left this one behind. I'm going to feed it."

"When it wakes up, dip the corner of a hankie into milk and let it suck," Mama suggested. "Tomorrow we'll see if Missy wants her little one back."

It was good to be in the quiet cabin with Mama. But Kirsten was much too excited to be able to sleep yet. She put the kitten in her lap, then laid her friendship quilt over her knees and tucked it close. After a moment the kitten began to purr.

Kirsten picked up the quilt square she hadn't been able to finish and started to sew her design again.

"What will you do with that square?" Mama asked in a sleepy voice.

Kirsten thought a moment. "I think I'll begin a quilt for our baby. It will take a long time to make, but that doesn't matter. I should have it finished before the weather gets cold again."

"What a special gift *that* will be," Mama said.

Kirsten smiled at Mama. "Remember you told me how glad you were to have a daughter? Is it better to have two daughters?"

Mama leaned to kiss Kirsten's cheek. "It's very good to have two daughters. But you are my only, only Kirsten. Happy birthday, dear."

LOOKING BACK 1854

A PEEK INTO
THE PAST

GROWING UP IN 1854

A family with a new baby

When American girls like Kirsten were growing up, babies were born at home. Doctors and hospitals were scarce on the frontier, so women called *midwives* helped mothers give birth to their babies. Older family members helped, too. Because people weren't as healthy and didn't know as much about medicine as we do today, it was more dangerous to have babies in 1854 than it is now. Most women had about seven children, but usually one or two of those children died.

The birth of a healthy baby was something to be thankful for. But keeping a baby healthy

54

wasn't easy. There was very little medicine available on the frontier, so many children died before their fifth birthdays from diseases that don't seem very serious today, like chicken pox, mumps, or measles.

Frontier stove

Frontier homes could be dangerous, too. Small children could easily burn themselves on hot stoves or fires. They could fall into uncovered wells or down the ladders or steps that led to cabin lofts and root cellars. But instead of putting up screens in front of open fireplaces or blocking steep stairways, parents taught young children to stay away from these things. They believed that the best way to keep children safe on the frontier was to teach them obedience. They thought children wouldn't get hurt if they did as they were told.

Children who were too young to learn obedience were protected in another way. Infants wore long dresses that trailed below their feet. These dresses made crawling around and getting into danger very difficult for them. Both boys and girls wore

A long baby dress

A boy wearing a dress

dresses until their third birthdays. Then boys were *shortened*—their mothers dressed them in short pants instead of dresses. Older children's clothes looked very much like their parents' clothes. Girls wore dresses that were just smaller versions of their mothers' dresses, and boys wore miniature versions of their fathers' pants and shirts. There were no children's styles like there are today.

There was not a lot of time for children to play in 1854. On the frontier, they worked hard at the same kinds of jobs their parents did. Very young children collected eggs and brought in wood chips to start the kitchen fire. By their ninth or tenth birthdays, girls helped their mothers in the house by cooking, sewing,

Girls doing chores

A corn-husking bee

and caring for their younger brothers and sisters. Boys helped their fathers by planting crops and taking care of the animals. When frontier girls reached their fourteenth birthdays, they had learned so much about housework that they were able to work for other families as hired girls or maids. Boys were able to do every farming chore.

Even though pioneer children had to work very hard to help their families, their parents tried to make work fun. Early settlers often invited neighbors for a *bee*—a social get-together to make quilts, husk corn, or raise a barn. Older children had nut and berry picking parties. Real parties, like

A quilting bee

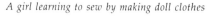
Children playing with homemade toys

birthday parties, were often simple family gatherings. Presents were inexpensive or practical things, like a piece of store-bought candy or a jackknife. Toys were often homemade. Girls played with rag dolls or dolls made from corncobs. They learned to sew by making their own doll clothes. Boys made their own bows and arrows, darts, and wooden whistles. Larger playthings like sleds, swings, and seesaws were handmade, too.

Although Kirsten's childhood sounds strict, she had much more freedom as a girl than she did as a grownup. In 1854, girls were allowed to show their lively spirits. They could play and go to school. Women had to control their spirits and be gentle and quiet. They

A girl learning to sew by making doll clothes

spent their time keeping house and raising children.

By the time she had her fifteenth or sixteenth birthday, a girl like Kirsten would be considered a woman. She would stop playing and going to school. She would wear her hair pulled back in a bun, and her skirts would reach the floor. She would start wearing corsets to make her look slim, and hoops to make her skirts stand out. She could marry and have a family of her own. If she didn't marry, she would probably live the rest of her life with her parents, caring and keeping house for them. Women like Miss Winston, who left home to teach school, were rare.

An 1850s bride

Children in the 1850s never asked themselves "What will I be when I grow up?" Girls like Kirsten knew they would be housewives with families like their mothers. Boys like Lars and Peter knew they would be farmers like their fathers. All their childhood experiences had trained them to do these jobs well.

Large families were common in the 1850s.